LOKSI' ISHKIN
HOMMA'

As told by Pauline Brown

Illustrated by Lauren John

Listen to this story in Chickasaw!

ISBN 978-1-952397-23-3 (hardcover)
ISBN 978-1-952397-24-0 (paperback)

Book design by Jackson Davis
Artwork by Lauren John
Printed in Canada

White Dog Press
c/o Chickasaw Press
PO Box 1548
Ada, Oklahoma 74821
chickasawpress.com

LOKSI' ISHKIN HOMMA'

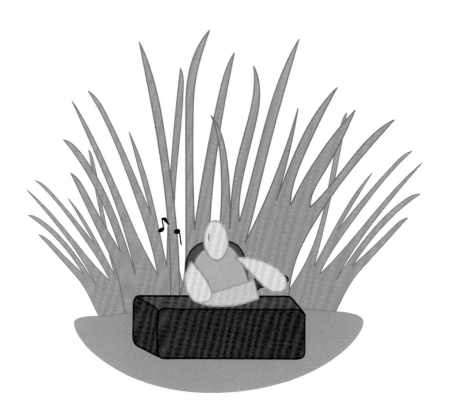

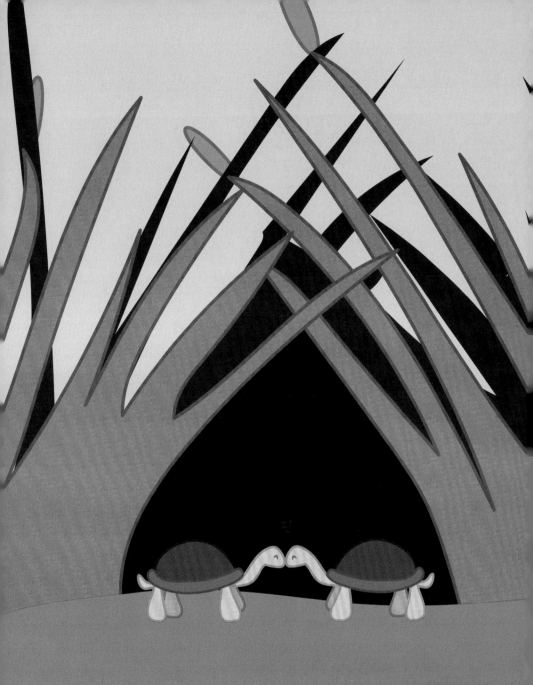

Chiiki mishshaash loksi' i̲hattak tá'at ás̲hwattook.

Hattak mat owwatta. Owwattat aya.

Yahmihm<u>a</u>, ihoo mat ishpiha' i'shcha pihlit ánta,
kaníhk<u>a</u> ayoppat, taloowat.

Yáhna, nakni' mat áana obya.

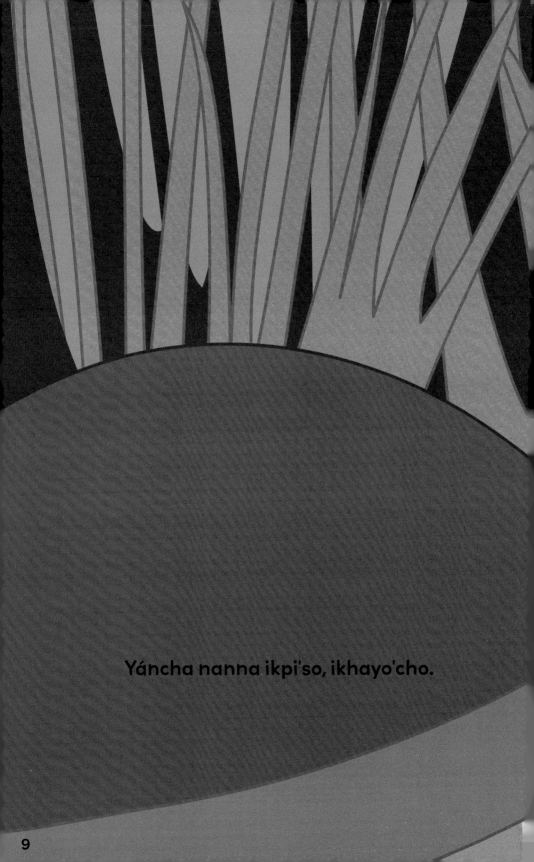

Yáncha nanna ikpi'so, ikhayo'cho.

Falamat míntik<u>a</u>, issishat bínni'tk<u>o</u>
"blood clot."

Haatok<u>o</u>, yamm<u>a</u> i'shcha, holisso áyya'shtok<u>o</u>, yamm<u>a</u> ishtakchit táyya'cha inchokka' m<u>a</u> ishto'nacha aaonao'si.

Pí'stokoot bashpo ma i'shcha
haloppachit ishtánta.

Yáhna, nakni' mat chokwaahmat, chokwaa. Yáhna
imihooat aachikat, "Ana' nipi'mano?" a'shna

"Yamma fokhilitok<u>o</u>, yamma tí'wa," a'shna

nipi' imahoobatok<u>o</u>, yamm<u>a</u> i' shcha
aaimpa' m<u>a</u> ishto'nacha

yamm<u>a</u> tiwwichit táyya'cha pisak<u>a</u>, issish
halalli' iskanno'si'at okaabínni'tokchaynina,

yamm<u>a</u> i'shcha, kan<u>í</u>hk<u>a</u> loksi' <u>i</u>nakni' m<u>a</u> ishkin finha okaaissona loksi' mat ittolat ántatok, aachi.

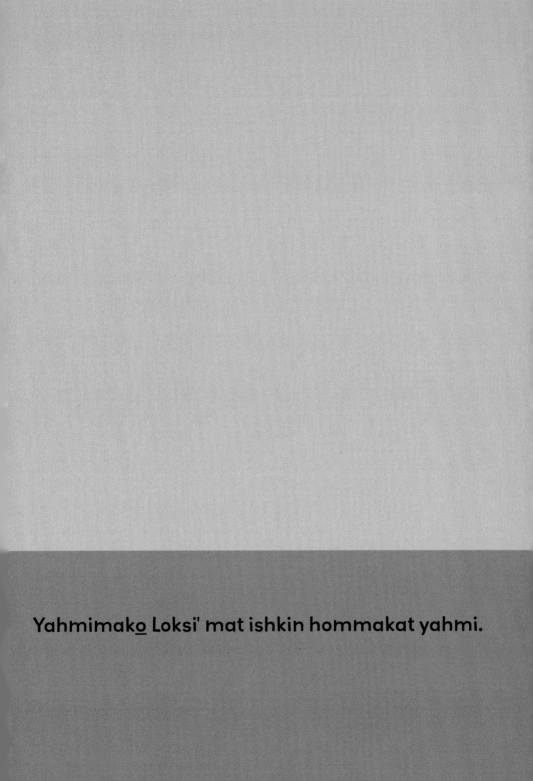

Yahmimak<u>o</u> Loksi' mat ishkin hommakat yahmi.

Yammak illa

Turtle's RED Eyes

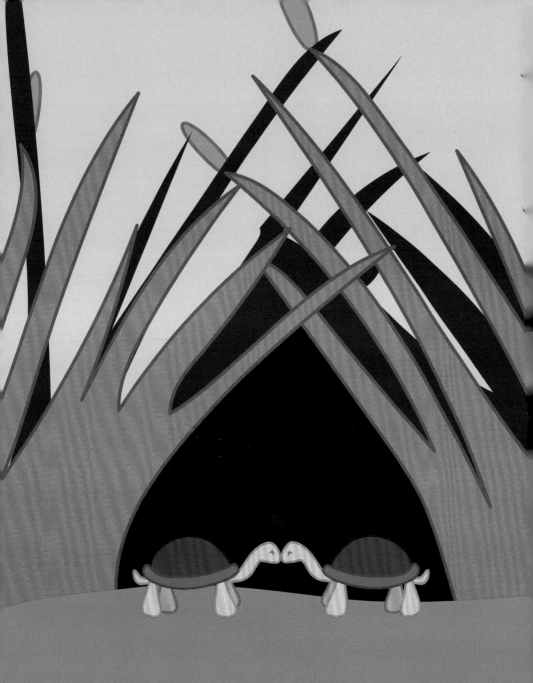

Long ago lived two happily married turtles.

One day, Turtle went hunting.

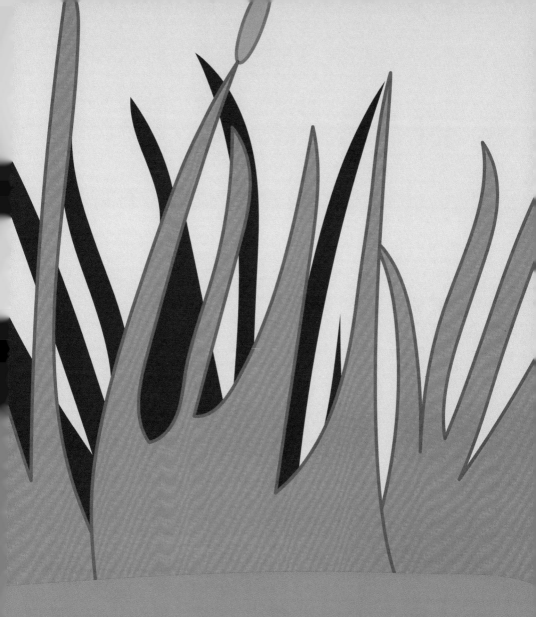

While he was away, his wife happily swept
their home and began singing.

Turtle was gone all day.

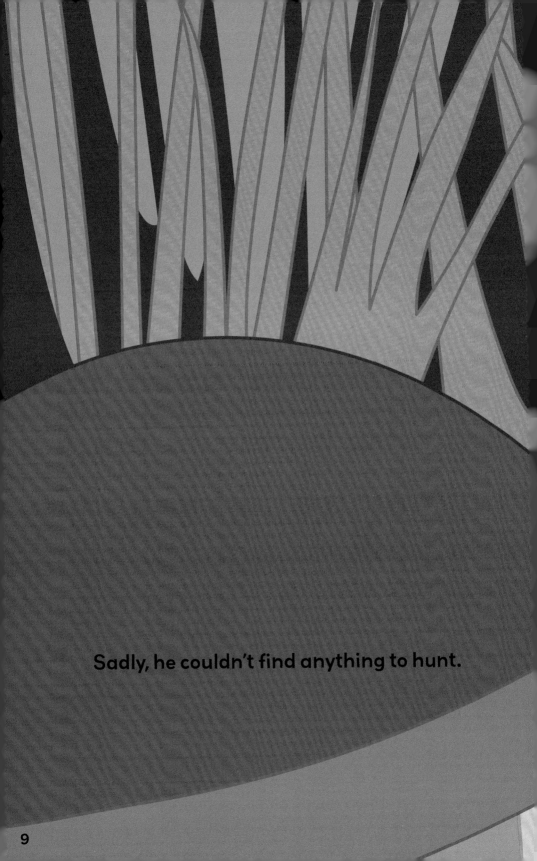

Sadly, he couldn't find anything to hunt.

As Turtle reluctantly made his way home, he noticed some blood on the ground—it was a blood clot!

Not wanting to go home empty-handed,
Turtle picked it up. He tied it in some paper
and carried it home.

As he arrived home, Turtle's wife saw the package.
She began to sharpen her knife.

As Turtle walked closer, his wife did not see any meat. Confused, she asked, "Where's my meat?"

"It's inside this paper wrapping," Turtle said.
So, Turtle's wife opened the package.

To her surprise, instead of meat she had
unwrapped a little bitty blood clot.

This was not meat!

Angry, she threw the clot right into Turtle's eyes.

And that's why Turtle has red eyes.

The End